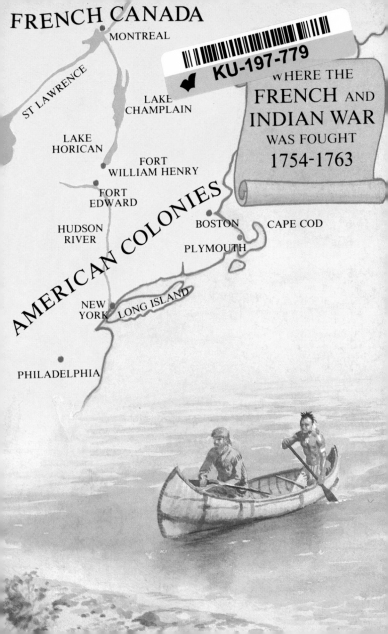

FRENCH CANADA

MONTREAL

ST LAWRENCE

LAKE CHAMPLAIN

LAKE HORICAN

FORT WILLIAM HENRY

FORT EDWARD

HUDSON RIVER

AMERICAN COLONIES

BOSTON

CAPE COD

PLYMOUTH

NEW YORK   LONG ISLAND

PHILADELPHIA

WHERE THE
FRENCH AND
INDIAN WAR
WAS FOUGHT
1754-1763

THIS LADYBIRD BOOK BELONGS TO:

_____

All Ladybird books are available at most bookshops,
supermarkets and newsagents, or can be ordered direct from:

Ladybird Postal Sales
PO Box 133 Paignton TQ3 2YP England
Telephone: (+44) 01803 554761
Fax: (+44) 01803 663394

A catalogue record for this book is available
from the British Library

Published by Ladybird Books Ltd
A subsidiary of the Penguin Group
A Pearson Company
© LADYBIRD BOOKS LTD MCMXCVII

LADYBIRD CLASSICS

THE LAST OF THE MOHICANS

by James Fenimore Cooper

Retold by Raymond Sibley
Illustrated by Frank Humphris

The Last of the Mohicans

Just over two hundred years ago, the Hudson River valley in North America was the scene of cruel and bitter fighting between the English and French settlers. Once the Mohican tribe of Indians had lived quietly in this valley. Now, the soldiers of England and France fought each other in the thick forests that separated the two sides. Many Indians from several different tribes were fighting too, some on one side and some on the other.

The English had a garrison at Fort Edward. In the year 1757, two young girls, Alice and Cora Munro, were waiting there to travel on to Fort William Henry, where their father, General Munro, commanded the English soldiers. This garrison was fifteen miles away at the head of the Horican Lake.

One morning an Indian runner called Magua arrived at Fort Edward with two messages. The first was that the French commander, Montcalm, was advancing with a large force. The second, that General Munro needed more men at Fort William Henry.

It was decided to send fifteen hundred soldiers to Fort William Henry early the next day, by the usual military route. Since the soldiers were likely to be attacked, Alice and

Cora would not be travelling with them. The sisters would go by horse, on a secret but more difficult path through the woods, with a young major called Duncan Heyward. The Indian messenger Magua was to be their guide.

Next morning they set off. The officer and the two girls were on horseback, and Magua led the way on foot. As they travelled along a dark narrow path through thick bushes, Alice, the younger sister, watched Magua closely. 'I don't trust him!' she whispered to Duncan Heyward.

'You may travel with the soldiers if you want to,' he replied, 'but their route is known to the enemy, while ours is still secret.'

'I'm sure we can trust him,' said Cora. She thought her sister was imagining things. But Alice was right to sense that they were not safe, for their father had once ordered Magua to be flogged for drunkenness. The young major knew of this, but had not told the two girls.

Magua was moving at a pace just above walking speed. He seemed to know the paths well, and the party followed him confidently, unaware that they themselves were being watched. They had travelled many miles when suddenly Magua slowed down, then stopped. 'We are lost,' he said. 'I can't find the next path.'

The sisters looked at each other, then at Major Heyward. 'What can we do?' asked Cora.

The major rode forward to look for himself. It was hopeless — thick bushes grew everywhere, and it was impossible to see ahead. Then, near the banks of a small stream, they came across three men.

One was an English frontier-scout, known as Hawk-eye. The others were Mohicans:

Chingachgook and his son Uncas. Hawk-eye
put his rifle across his left arm and kept his
right forefinger on the trigger as Major
Heyward rode towards him. 'We are lost. Can
you direct us to the fort called William
Henry?' asked the major.

Hawk-eye laughed. 'You are very far off the track. It will be easier for you to follow the river to Fort Edward.'

'We left there this morning,' said Heyward, 'with our Indian guide.'

Hawk-eye looked suspicious. 'An Indian lost in the woods?' he said disbelievingly. 'That is very strange. What tribe is he?'

'He is a Huron called Magua.'

'A Huron,' repeated Hawk-eye. 'They are treacherous and cannot be trusted. Let me have a look at this guide.'

The frontier-scout turned to look at Magua, who was leaning against a tree a little distance away, a cruel look on his face.

'If I go towards him,' said Hawk-eye, 'he will suspect something and run away through the trees. It would be better to let Chingachgook and Uncas capture him from behind.'

But just as Hawk-eye finished speaking, Magua turned suddenly and disappeared into the woods. The speed with which he moved took them by surprise and though they searched he was not to be found.

Now Heyward's party had no guide and no protection — and they were lost! The young major thought for a few minutes, then asked the frontier-scout if he and the two Indians would escort them to Fort William Henry.

Heyward promised to pay whatever they asked. After they had talked the matter over, Hawk-eye and the two Mohicans agreed.

The shadows of the evening were beginning to lengthen, so Hawk-eye pulled a bark canoe from the bushes at the edge of the river. The two girls got into it, while the Mohicans took their horses along the bank of the river to hide them until morning.

The little party paddled the canoe a short distance along the river, until they reached Glenn's Falls. Here they stepped out onto the rocks, where they were soon joined by Chingachgook and Uncas.

Hawk-eye and the two Indians went to find a cave where they could spend the night. They returned quickly, to lead the party to a big cave within sound of a rumbling waterfall. The Mohicans had brought venison and salt with them, and the scout made a fire to cook a meal. Uncas served the ladies, although usually Indian custom forbade warriors to wait on women.

He and his father Chingachgook were very much alike, but Alice was impressed by the young man's proud bearing. She said to Cora, 'I shall sleep soundly with such a fearless warrior to protect me!'

When everyone had eaten, the entrance to the cave was concealed with some branches, and they prepared for sleep. The sisters rested peacefully in each other's arms, while the men took it in turn to keep guard.

Near dawn Hawk-eye shook Duncan Heyward awake, and told him he was going to bring the canoe to the landing place. The two Indians would remain on guard in front of the cave. When Hawk-eye had gone, Heyward decided to wake the sisters up, but before he could do so, there came loud yells and cries from outside the cave, followed by the sound of rifle fire!

For almost a minute the air was filled with frightening noise. Magua had returned with other members of the Huron tribe.

As Chingachgook and Uncas fired back at their enemies, Duncan Heyward watched for the return of Hawk-eye with the canoe. Then Hawk-eye came back, and with his first shot he killed one of their attackers. At this the other Hurons retreated, and silence returned.

'Back into the cave,' said Hawk-eye. 'The Hurons will attack again soon. There are about forty of them.'

The men then primed their pistols for, as Hawk-eye told them, the mist from the waterfall could dampen the powder.

Suddenly four Indians rushed from cover and made for the cave. Chingachgook and Uncas fired, and the two men in the lead fell to the ground. The other two hurled themselves upon Hawk-eye and Heyward.

Hawk-eye stabbed his attacker to the heart. Heyward struggled desperately with the other. They fought to the edge of the rocks, beyond which was a sheer drop to certain death. Just as Heyward felt they would both go over, he saw the knife of Uncas come down. His enemy released his grip and fell from sight over the edge.

'Come back to cover!' shouted Hawk-eye.

When they were all together again Uncas and Duncan Heyward looked at one another, then clasped hands in friendship.

As they did so, a shot rang out, the bullet striking a rock near Heyward's side. It was fired by an Indian who had climbed an oak tree on the opposite bank. They all took cover and waited. A long time went by before the Huron revealed himself and attempted another shot. When he appeared, Hawk-eye took careful aim and fired. The Indian fell into the foaming waters of the river.

Immediately Hawk-eye sent Uncas to the canoe for more powder for their rifles. But the canoe was being pulled away by a Huron, swimming hidden on its far side.

'Since we have no gunpowder, our rifles are useless now,' said Hawk-eye. 'We shall all die, because every path out of here will be watched. The only escape is by swimming downriver with the current. But we cannot leave the ladies.'

'You will have to,' said Cora. 'Duncan can stay with us here, and you three can escape and bring help from my father at Fort William Henry.'

After much talk and argument it was agreed that this was the best plan. One by one the men dropped into the stream and went with the current. The two sisters went back into the cave with Duncan Heyward. 'We shall be secret and safe,' said Alice, 'for even if the Hurons come back, they will not find us here.'

But they had not been long in the cave when they heard the sound of Huron voices outside. After some minutes of mutterings from the next cave, there was silence. Suddenly there was a rush. They were overpowered and dragged outside.

Magua looked down at them. 'Where are the bodies of the scout and the Mohicans?' he asked.

'They are not dead. They have escaped and gone to bring help,' said Duncan.

The Hurons rushed to the river and yelled with anger when they saw their three enemies had escaped. This made them look at Duncan, Alice and Cora with even more menace. But Magua had them under tight control. He issued orders and the three white people were taken across the river in a canoe.

On the opposite bank they were pushed out, and the Hurons split into two groups. Magua kept five men with him to guard the prisoners.

There were two horses, and Duncan helped Alice and Cora onto their backs. Magua led the way and they set off. After a long walk, the Hurons stopped to eat. Magua told Duncan to send Cora to him.

Cora had no idea why Magua wished to see her, so she stood before him in silence, waiting for him to speak.

'Daughter of Munro,' he said at last, 'your

father once said that no Indian on his camp should swallow firewater. But a white man gave some to Magua, and so your father had me tied to a post and flogged like a dog. On my back − the back of a Huron chief − are the scars of which I am ashamed.'

'Why are you telling me this?' asked Cora.

'I want you to live in my wigwam as my wife, so that Munro knows his daughter is fetching water for Magua, cooking his food and cleaning his wigwam. This would make Munro sad.'

'I shall never do that!' replied Cora.

Magua looked coldly into her eyes, then he turned to the other Hurons. As he spoke they grew more and more angry until they hurled themselves at Duncan, Alice and Cora, dragged them away and tied them to trees. Once they were secure, the Hurons stood back.

Suddenly, with a loud scream, Magua threw his tomahawk. It struck the tree above Alice's head, cutting off some strands of her hair. This maddened Duncan, who broke loose and leapt at the Huron who was preparing to throw next. They fell together but just as the Indian raised his knife, the crack of a rifle was heard and the Huron dropped dead.

Magua and the four remaining Indians were taken completely by surprise as Hawk-eye, Chingachgook and Uncas ran out from behind the thicket. Duncan Heyward leapt forward too, and a violent fight took place. Four of the Hurons were killed within minutes, and Magua sank to the ground from a heavy blow by Chingachgook.

Alice and Cora put their arms around each other, weeping with the relief of being saved from death.

Hawk-eye told Duncan that they had heard the Hurons yelling around the caves, so they had returned, watched, and followed at a safe distance, waiting for the right moment to attack. While he was telling the story, Magua, who had been pretending, got to his feet and ran into the bushes out of sight. The Mohicans would have followed, but Hawk-eye stopped them.

Soon the party moved back to where the two horses were standing, and Alice and Cora mounted. They set off once more in the direction of Fort William, with Hawk-eye in the lead. As darkness fell, he took them to a crumbling, tumbledown building, hidden in the trees, which he had remembered. 'We can rest here,' he said.

Hardly had they settled down before Chingachgook, who was on first watch, said that he could hear enemies outside in the darkness. 'Bring the horses in here,' whispered Hawk-eye, 'and everyone keep still.'

About twenty Hurons were moving about outside. Gradually they got nearer to the building until it seemed they must hear the horses breathing. Inside, the party waited nervously as the minutes passed. Then the sounds from the Hurons began to grow fainter. There were some burial mounds outside the building, and in respect for the dead the Hurons had moved away.

At last all was still. As soon as the Mohicans were sure it was safe, the whole party crept in the darkness to the banks of the stream. Here the two girls again mounted the horses.

'Now we walk along in the water,' said Hawk-eye, 'for that way we shall leave no trail.'

This they did for about an hour, until they came to a sandy bank with many trees. They left the water, and Hawk-eye led the way once more.

'It is a long and weary path from here to Fort William Henry,' he said, 'but I know the way very well. We must keep to the west, go through the mountains, and watch all the time for Montcalm's French soldiers.'

On they went — slowly, for ragged rocks and steep slopes made the route difficult. When they reached a flat and mossy summit, Hawk-eye told the sisters to get off their horses.

'We must let the horses loose here,' he told them. 'They can go no further.'

From the top of the hill they could see the southern shore of Horican Lake below, and towards the west were the buildings of Fort William Henry. But all eyes went straight to the artillery of General Montcalm, who had moved his forces very close to the fort.

'Don't worry,' Hawk-eye said to the girls. 'The Mohicans and I will lead you to your father. There is a fog coming down which will help.'

They followed him down the steep slope until they reached level ground. By this time the fog was rolling down quickly, and they waited until it covered the camp of the enemy.

'We must move with care,' said Hawk-eye, 'for they have posted guards, both redskin and white.'

As they crept slowly through the fog, they heard all kinds of sounds: voices in French; voices in the Huron tongue; and the sounds of firing, both of musket and cannon ball. And all the time Hawk-eye was edging them closer and closer to the fort.

Suddenly the small group heard a voice above them. It was General Munro, the girls' father! Alice and Cora shouted through the fog to him, and within seconds some soldiers came out of the fort to help them in. It all happened with breathtaking speed.

The girls and their father were so overjoyed to see one another that in the days following they forgot the danger they were in. They forgot Montcalm, and the French soldiers, and the Indian warriors covering the fort.

Although they knew that they were in constant physical danger while the siege lasted, they forgot that too. Munro was almost defenceless, and was still waiting hopefully for Webb to arrive from Fort Edward with reinforcements.

About the third day, Montcalm sent word that he was prepared to talk. General Munro decided to send Major Duncan Heyward as his agent, and Duncan left the fort with a white flag of truce. He was met by a French officer who took him to General Montcalm.

When Duncan entered the French commander's tent, he looked around with interest. Montcalm was with his senior French officers and some Indian chiefs — including Magua! The French general was very polite.

'Your leader is brave,' he said, 'but to save bloodshed, would it not be better to surrender to me now? I cannot hold back the anger of these Indians for much longer. If I let them, they will butcher you all. So let us speak of terms.'

'A powerful force is on its way to help us,' replied Duncan — and did not understand why Montcalm smiled.

They talked for a long time, but neither would give way, and at last Duncan stood up to leave. Then Montcalm showed him a letter captured from a messenger. It was written by General Webb who was expected to bring the relief force from Fort Edward. Montcalm showed it to Duncan who exclaimed in amazement, 'That is Webb's signature!'

The letter was addressed to Munro and stated that it was impossible to send any more men to help him. It advised him to surrender Fort William Henry immediately. Duncan was downcast, but General Montclam was generous. 'I shall allow you all to leave with your weapons intact, and the King's colours, in an honourable and soldierly manner. Then I shall destroy the fort. You will not be harmed.'

When Duncan reported to Munro, the general accepted Montcalm's conditions. He signed a treaty agreeing to leave the fort next morning.

One who was *not* pleased was Magua, the Huron chief. 'Now the English are leaving,' he

muttered, 'the French no longer call them
enemies. But they are still *my* enemies, and I
will be revenged on them.'

The next day the English soldiers marched in
formation to the French lines, to make their
official surrender. Some time later, the women
and the wounded moved out, accompanied by
a handful of soldiers.

When they had walked a short distance
from the fort, Cora noticed that Magua and
the Hurons were watching a group of women
who were beginning to fall behind the rest of
the party. The French, under Montcalm, were
a good distance away.

Suddenly a Huron ran and pulled a baby from its mother's arms, beat the child's head against a rock, threw the body down, and drove a tomahawk into the mother's brain. At this Magua gave a signal, and from the forest came more than two thousand Huron warriors, who rushed to the attack. While the cruel slaying of the defenceless went on, the sights and sounds of death were everywhere.

Magua himself took Alice and Cora as his prisoners. 'Come,' he said to Cora, 'my wigwam is still open to you.' She stood silent, sickened by the blood which covered his hands and arms. He dragged them to the trees, put them both on the same horse (for Alice had fainted) and led them along a trail through the forest. They stopped at the same high place where Hawk-eye had taken them, several days before.

From here they looked down at the killing on the plain below, for the Hurons did not cease until the slaughter was complete. After a long time, the cries of the wounded, the shrieks of horror and the yells of the murderers grew less and less until at last all was quiet.

Later still Hawk-eye, Chingachgook, Uncas, Munro and Heyward searched for the bodies of Alice and Cora. Controlling their feelings of horror, they looked closely at all the dead women, one by one. It was a sickening task. Then on a bush Uncas found a piece of the green veil that Cora had been wearing.

'She is alive!' said the general joyfully.

'Yes,' replied Hawk-eye, 'and with care, and if we go softly, we shall be able to follow her trail. But we must be patient.'

Chingachgook, examining the spot closely, added, 'Magua is with her.'

Progress was slow and painstaking but soon they found part of a necklace, and were encouraged. Heyward recognised it at once. It belonged to Alice. Her father's eyes filled with tears when he saw it.

As darkness came they had a meal of dried bear's meat, and rested, not far from the ruined fort. When Hawk-eye woke Duncan Heyward and Munro next morning he said, 'We must take great care, for we now have enemies both in front of us and behind us.'

Uncas and Chingachgook had gone to fetch a canoe from the edge of the lake near the

fort. When they returned, the party got into the canoe and paddled out over the calm waters of the Horican Lake. They kept close to the banks and little wooded islands for cover, and by late afternoon they had reached the northern end of the lake. The canoe was lifted from the water and the men carried it into the trees. Then they left a false trail, for when they came to a stream they walked back in the water to the lake before launching the canoe again, and paddling towards the western shore. Here the canoe was taken ashore and carefully hidden under a pile of branches before the party made camp.

In the morning, Hawk-eye led the way towards a forest. It was a wild region, but he and the two Indians knew it well.

They walked several miles without finding any trace of the girls, then Uncas pointed to the side of the trail. 'See,' he said, 'they have taken them further into the forest.'

Slowly they went on. Magua and his men had also left some false trails and turnings, but the three trackers were not fooled. By early afternoon they came to a large stream and the party walked along, in the water, until the evening.

As night came on, they reached a clearing in the trees where there stood about a hundred earth lodges, with several Indians moving around. The little party stayed out of sight, and after some talk it was decided that Chingachgook should take Munro to a small hiding-place he knew of nearby and guard him there. Hawk-eye and Uncas were to separate to spy out as much as they could about what the Hurons were doing.

Duncan Heyward then offered to do a very dangerous thing. He suggested that he be painted up, by Chingachgook, to look like one of the many entertainers who moved from camp to camp. His knowledge of French would help to convince the Hurons of his friendliness. Once in the camp he could search for Cora and Alice. His friends were not convinced, but Duncan was stubborn and insisted, 'If they are somewhere in that village, I must try to free them, whatever the danger.'

So Chingachgook painted Duncan's face, with great skill, and soon the young major looked the part of a juggler. Hawk-eye told him what signals they would use, and where they would meet later. Once they were all clear as to their tasks, Uncas disappeared into the trees in search of Magua. Hawk-eye went off in a different direction.

As he walked into the camp, Duncan felt more keenly the dangers of his mission. It was by then quite dark. When he reached the earth lodges, he was met by children who peered at him but said nothing. In the centre of the village, some of the elders were sitting near a flaming torch. One of them looked like a chief. He spoke in Huron; Duncan replied in French. The chief then asked Duncan, in French, why he had entered the camp with his face painted.

'When an Indian chief visits his white friends, he takes off his buffalo robe and wears the shirt given him,' said Duncan. 'My Indian friends gave me paint to wear, when I visit their tribes.'

The elders were very pleased with this compliment and Duncan was invited to sit with them and chat. Half an hour passed and Duncan began to feel the strain. While they were speaking there arose a yelling in the forest, and a line of warriors came from the trees carrying scalps on a long pole. All the men in the village drew their knives and the squaws and children seized clubs and axes, before forming two lines. The war party marched between these lines into the middle of the camp, bringing two prisoners. The two men were mocked, tormented and struck as

they were pushed towards one of the earth
lodges. There they were both tied to posts.

As the torches flickered in the darkness,
Duncan found the scene hideous and
frightening. He worked his way near to the
two captives and one of them turned his head
and looked at Duncan with firm piercing eyes.
It was Uncas!

The other captive was a Huron who had turned coward in the previous fight. After being insulted and shamed by words, he was stabbed in the heart with a hunting-knife. Immediately all the torches in the lodge were dashed into the earth, burying everything in darkness. In the few seconds before he was jostled away, Duncan heard Uncas whisper that Hawk-eye was still free.

Outside the lodge a warrior approached Duncan with a strange request.

'There is an evil spirit in my wife,' he said. 'Can you use your medicine to frighten it away?'

Now Duncan knew a little about Indian customs and he felt it would be a good excuse to move around the camp, so he agreed. The Huron walked towards the edge of the village. 'Come, follow me,' he said. Then he pointed at Uncas.

'The Mohican will die in the morning,' he said. 'The sun will shine on his shame and the squaws will see his flesh tremble.'

On their way to the Huron's sick wife, they went by a bear which was at the side of the path. Indians often kept tamed bears near the camp so Duncan was not afraid. It seemed to take little notice of them, but as soon as they had gone by, it followed them at a distance.

The Huron stopped near some openings in the rocks. Through one of these was the sick woman. She had been put there by the Indians who thought that the spirit would have more difficulty getting through stone walls to torment her.

Duncan insisted that the Indian left him alone with the woman, who seemed to be in a deep sleep. Once he had gone Duncan began to look about him.

Suddenly the bear appeared in the stone doorway. It lifted its head to one side — it was Hawk-eye inside the skin! When Duncan had recovered from the shock, Hawk-eye explained that he had seen one of the Indian conjurors in the woods, preparing to get into the bearskin. He had overpowered the man and tied him to a tree. Then he had put on the bearskin himself.

'After spending years in the wild, I know the nature and movements of animals very well,' he added.

'What have you found out?' asked Duncan.

'The fair one, Alice, is on the other side of this wall. You must go to her, for the sight of me as a bear would frighten her. You had better rub off some of your paint first.'

After he had done this, Duncan went in to Alice. Although she was very relieved to be rescued, she was very pale and nervous. He told her that her father was safe, and then he asked where Cora was.

'She has been taken to another place by Magua.'

Duncan picked up some Indian blankets. 'I will wrap you in these and carry you outside. The Hurons will think you are the sick woman.'

Outside in the darkness, some of the Hurons were still waiting. 'Where are you taking her?' asked the husband.

'I have shut the evil spirit in the rocks,' replied Duncan. 'Now I am taking her into the woods to give her some strengthening roots to eat. I will return her to your wigwam when the sun comes again.' With that he left them. When he was some distance from the village, Duncan put Alice down. Hawk-eye joined them and pointed out the path to safety.

'If you meet any of the Delawares, they will help you, for their tribe and the Mohicans are the same people and the same stock. They are all children of the tortoise.'

'What about you?' asked Alice.

'I shall go back and free Uncas,' said Hawk-eye.

They parted, and Hawk-eye, still in the bear costume, made his way back to the village. Although the Hurons had gone into their lodges for the night there was, nevertheless, great danger. There were two warriors near the lodge where Uncas was captive, and Hawk-eye waited in hiding for many long minutes until they had moved away and all was quiet.

At first Uncas thought his enemies had sent a beast to torment him, until he realised it was Hawk-eye. As soon as he had been cut loose, he whispered to Hawk-eye, 'We must make for the Delawares, for they are the children of my grandfathers and will help us.'

Stealthily they moved through the camp and into the trees, moving towards the distant fires of the Delaware tribe. They walked all through the night. As day began to dawn they came up with Alice and Duncan Heyward — together they moved on, until they reached the children of the tortoise.

Later that morning when Tamenund, the wise man of the Delawares, saw Uncas for the first time, his eyes opened wide. He pointed to the beautifully tattooed blue tortoise on the young Mohican's chest and asked, 'Who are you?'

'I am Uncas, the son of Chingachgook, son of the great turtle, Unamis. The blood of the turtle has been in many chiefs, but all are dead, except my father and myself.'

'Then you are the last of the Mohicans?' said Tamenund.

'I am,' said Uncas proudly.

Tamenund was so happy to hear this that he offered the best of the Delaware warriors to track down Magua and rescue Cora.

'Our spies say he is not far from here, with some of the Hurons. They have put the maiden into one of the caves, under guard.'

So it was decided that Uncas, because he was the last of his tribe, should attack the

main force of the Hurons with the Delawares,
while Hawk-eye, with twenty men and rifles,
should go by another route to pick up Munro
and Chingachgook. They would join Uncas
near the cave where Cora was being held.

When he was fully prepared, Hawk-eye led
his small band of braves out of the camp and
along a stream. All seemed quiet and peaceful
in the trees, and at the beaver lodges they
met Munro and Chingachgook. By this time
they could hear the sounds of battle in the
distance. Slowly and quietly they moved
towards the denser and darker part of the
forest where the heavy fighting was taking
place, and where they knew Cora was held
captive.

When the party came within sight of the caves, they saw that Uncas and his followers had burst through the Huron lines, forcing them to retreat. At the thought of Cora, Duncan Heyward pushed past Hawk-eye and rushed towards the caves. Once inside, he searched desperately for the girl.

Then in one of the gloomy passages he found himself side by side with the fighting Uncas. Several paces away they caught sight of Cora's white robe, for Magua and another Huron were pulling her along with them.

Uncas threw down his rifle and leapt towards her. As he reached Magua, the other

Huron pushed his knife into Cora's heart. At the moment she fell, Uncas stumbled and Magua buried his tomahawk in the Mohican's body. Uncas turned to strike down Cora's murderer, but the effort was his last. Now he faced Magua, who drove his knife three times into the Mohican's heart.

These deaths happened with such speed that Duncan had barely reached the bodies of Cora and Uncas when Magua ran out to the edge of the rock. There he made an enormous leap over a wide drop to reach the safety of the other side. He fell short, but grasped a shrub in an attempt to lift himself. Hawk-eye aimed his rifle and fired. The body of Magua fell to its destruction, and soon afterwards the sounds of the fighting came to an end.

As the sun rose next day, with the battle over and the Hurons beaten, many wept for those who had died. The bodies of Cora and Uncas were on the ground. They had been prepared for burial and were covered in flowers, ornaments, bracelets and medals.

But Chingachgook said, 'Why do you mourn and weep? They died bravely! My boy is dead. All my race have gone now. I am alone.'

'No,' said Hawk-eye. 'You are not alone.'

He stretched out his hand, and Chingachgook grasped it firmly in deep friendship. Their heads bowed, while burning tears fell on the body of Uncas, the last of the Mohicans.

Munro never recovered from the shock of his daughter's death. Alice returned to England with Duncan Heyward, and Chingachgook lived on for many years, with his friend Hawk-eye never far away.

LAKE
ONTARIO